This book belongs to

_____

WALT DISNEY®

CHOOSE YOUR OWN ADVENTURE®

WIND IN THE WILLOWS ADVENTURE

Story adapted by JIM RAZZI

Bantam **Books**

TORONTO • NEW YORK • LONDON • SYDNEY • AUCKLAND

RL 2, 004–008

WIND IN THE WILLOWS ADVENTURE

A Bantam Book / December 1986

*CHOOSE YOUR OWN ADVENTURE® is a registered trademark
of Bantam Books, Inc. Registered in U.S. Patent and
Trademark Office and elsewhere.*

*Concept: Edward Packard; Series Development:
R.A. Montgomery and Edward Packard.*

Library of Congress Cataloging-in-Publication Data

Razzi, Jim.
  Wind in the willows adventure.

  (Walt Disney choose your own adventure)
  Summary: The reader's decisions control a series of
adventures with four animal friends who live along a
river in the English countryside.
  1. Plot-your-own stories. [1. Animals—Fiction.
2. Plot-your-own stories] I. Graham, Kenneth, 1859–
1932. Wind in the willows. II. Title. III. Series.
PZ7.R233Wi 1986   [E]   86-14180
ISBN 0-553-05419-8

Published simultaneously in the United States and Canada

---

*Bantam Books are published by Bantam Books, Inc. Its trade-
mark, consisting of the words "Bantam Books" and the portrayal
of a rooster, is Registered in U.S. Patent and Trademark Office
and in other countries. Marca Registrada. Bantam Books, Inc.,
666 Fifth Avenue, New York, New York 10103.*

PRINTED IN THE UNITED STATES OF AMERICA

DW   0 9 8 7 6 5 4 3 2 1

Classic® binding, R. R. Donnelley & Sons Company. U.S. Patent
No. 4,408,780; Patented in Canada 1984; Patents in other
countries issued or pending.

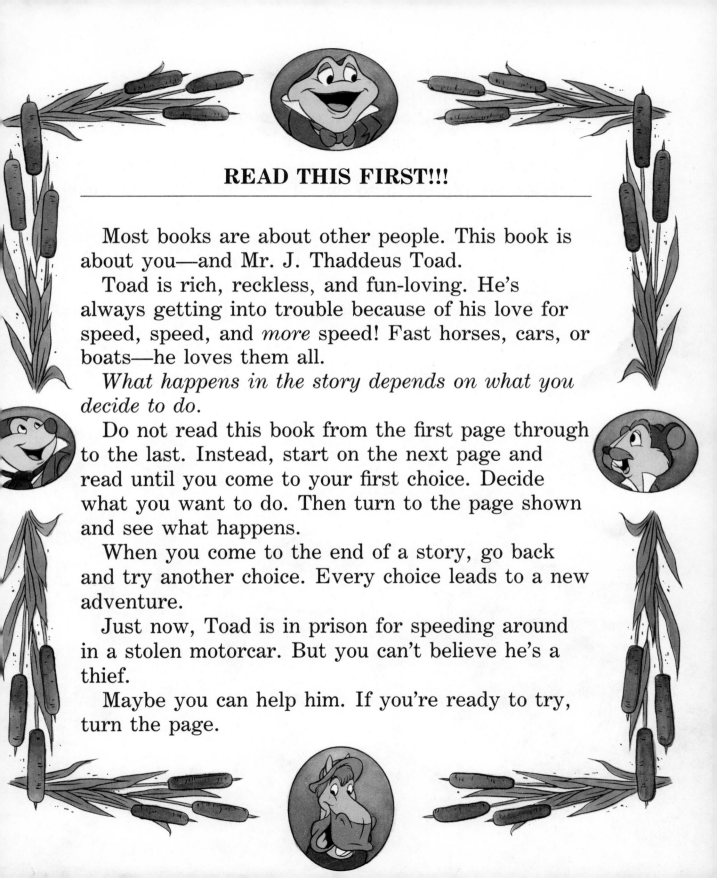

READ THIS FIRST!!!

Most books are about other people. This book is about you—and Mr. J. Thaddeus Toad.

Toad is rich, reckless, and fun-loving. He's always getting into trouble because of his love for speed, speed, and *more* speed! Fast horses, cars, or boats—he loves them all.

What happens in the story depends on what you decide to do.

Do not read this book from the first page through to the last. Instead, start on the next page and read until you come to your first choice. Decide what you want to do. Then turn to the page shown and see what happens.

When you come to the end of a story, go back and try another choice. Every choice leads to a new adventure.

Just now, Toad is in prison for speeding around in a stolen motorcar. But you can't believe he's a thief.

Maybe you can help him. If you're ready to try, turn the page.

You're riding along an open country road one evening with your friend Cyril the horse.

"It's a crime that Toad is in jail," says Cyril. "He's completely innocent of stealing that motorcar!"

"I think so, too," you say.

"I *know* he's innocent!" exclaims Cyril. "Because I was there when he bought that car."

"Really?" you say.

"Yes," Cyril answers. "This is what happened . . ."

Go on to the next page.

"One day," Cyril begins, "Toad and I see this lovely red motorcar outside a tavern. It looks *fast*, so naturally Toad wants to buy it . . ."

"Naturally," you say.

"We go inside the tavern," Cyril continues, "and the owner—Winkey was his name—says the car belongs to a pack of weasels sitting right there."

"What happened then?" you ask.

"Well, it seems that Toad had no money."

Turn to page 2.

You nod—you know why Toad had no money.

Since Toad spent money the same way he did everything else—speedily—his old friend MacBadger was handling his money for him.

"Yes," says Cyril. "MacBadger wouldn't give Toad another cent to spend until he mended his ways."

"Then how did he pay for the motorcar?" you ask.

Go on to the next page.

"Ah!" cries Cyril. "In exchange for the motorcar, he gave those weasels an important piece of paper—the deed to Toad Hall."

You gasp. Toad Hall is Toad's home. It's the grandest house on the river. It's worth a fortune!

"But the sad fact," Cyril says, "is that the police didn't believe that Toad bought the car from the weasels—and with Toad Hall of all things!"

Turn to page 4.

4   "But if we could get the deed back," you cry,
"Toad could prove his story is true!"

Just then, you reach the top of a hill. Ahead of
you on the road are your good friends Rat and
Mole.

"Hello," you call as Cyril comes to a stop.

"How d'you do," replies Rat, nodding politely.

"Hello there!" says Mole with a smile.

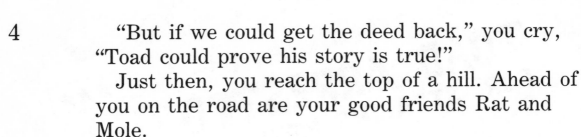

Go on to the next page.

"Ahem," says Rat. "Seeing as how we've bumped into each other, would you and Cyril like to come over for a visit?"

You would love to visit along the riverbank with Rat and Mole. But you had planned to go to town with Cyril.

What should you do?

If you decide to join Rat and Mole, turn to page 6.

If you and Cyril head into town, turn to page 8.

"Thank you," you say to Rat. "I'd enjoy a visit."
Cyril says that he must go into town.

You and Rat and Mole wave good-bye to him.

Later that evening, you and your friends are
seated at a small table with a fine supper spread
before you.

You all have been trying very hard to be merry,
but your thoughts keep returning to poor Toad.

"It's terrible that he's in prison," says Rat.

Go on to the next page.

"But Toad says he didn't steal that motorcar!" cries Mole. "He bought it from the weasels."

"Quite so," sniffs Rat in a disbelieving way.

All of a sudden, the door behind you swings open.

You peer around the wing of your chair and see a little old lady. But wait! It's really Toad in disguise! He must have escaped from prison!

Turn to page 10.

"I'm sorry, but I have things to do in town," you say. "Thank you for the invitation, anyway."

You and Cyril wave good-bye to Rat and Mole and head into town.

"I've been thinking," you say to Cyril. "There must be something we can do to help Toad."

Go on to the next page.

"There is," replies Cyril with a wink. "I have a plan for freeing Toad from prison!"

"You do?" you say.

"That's right!" cries Cyril. "I was going to do it on my own, but it'll work better with you along."

"Great!" you shout. "I'm ready whenever you are!"

Turn to page 14.

"Toad, how—" you start to say. Suddenly Mac-Badger barges into the house.

He looks shocked to see Toad, but he's very excited about something.

"I've just found out that Toad *is* innocent!" he announces.

"I knew it!" you cry.

"So did I," cries Mole. "But what proof do you have?"

Go on to the next page.

"I've been to Toad Hall. A pack of weasels and a fellow named Winkey have moved in there!" continues MacBadger. "So Toad *did* buy the motorcar from the weasels. And he paid for it with Toad Hall!"

"Winkey! I bet he's the weasels' leader!" cries Toad, quickly pulling off his disguise. "And he must have the deed I gave them!"

"Well, what are we waiting for?" you say. "Let's go to Toad Hall and get back that deed!"

Turn to page 12.

12 You all hop into a rowboat and quietly make your way along the river. Soon you arrive at Toad Hall.

Before you is the entrance to a secret underground tunnel. It leads right into Toad's home.

"Maybe someone should stay here on the riverbank and guard the boat while the others go ahead," says MacBadger softly.

You're the biggest. Should you be the guard? Or would you be more help inside Toad Hall?

If you decide to guard the boat, turn to page 15.

If you want to take the secret tunnel, turn to page 19.

14   Later that night, you and Cyril arrive at Toad's new home—the prison.

Cyril is wearing a dress and a wig.

"Now, dearie," says Cyril in a high voice, "why don't you talk to this nice officer while I visit my grandson, Toad."

You know the plan is for you to keep the guard busy. But now you wonder if Cyril will need your help inside. Should you go with him?

If you stay with the guard, turn to page 22.

If you go with Cyril, turn to page 27.

"I'll stay with the boat," you whisper.

The others nod and creep into the tunnel. You watch them until they're out of sight.

All of a sudden, a weasel guard sees you. He races toward you!

Quickly you untie the boat and push off into the river. The weasel makes a grab for the boat. He misses and grabs one of your oars instead!

Turn to page 16.

16   The river's current is strong, and with only one oar, you're helpless. You have no way to steer.

The boat picks up speed. It's traveling faster and faster!

Go on to the next page.

Then you remember why the current is so strong. There's a waterfall downriver!

And you're heading straight for it!

You grip the sides of the boat. Now the river is moving so fast that the water is white with foam.

You bounce and scrape over rocks as you speed toward the roaring falls.

Turn to page 18.

18   You look around wildly.

You see that the trees along the bank bend their branches over the water.

You'd better grab one of those branches before you reach the falls. If you don't, the river and you are going to come to the same .

.

**E
n
d**

"I think we should *all* go to Toad Hall!" you say.
The others agree.

The secret tunnel leads to a hidden door. You
open it and tiptoe inside. Winkey and the weasels
are lying all over the place, snoring away.

"Now's the time to look for the deed," says
MacBadger.

"There it is!" you whisper, pointing.

MacBadger groans. "It's in Winkey's pocket!"

Turn to page 20.

20   In a flash, you all run up to the balcony, just above Winkey.

MacBadger attaches a rope to Mole. He lowers Mole over the side so that he can grab the deed out of Winkey's pocket.

As you watch nervously you feel your nose becoming itchy.

Oh, no. You're going to—"ACHOO!"—sneeze!

Go on to the next page.

Your loud sneeze wakes everyone up.

Winkey checks his pocket. "The deed! It's gone!"
he yells.

Then he sees you and the others dashing down
the stairs.

"Get them, you blokes!" he shouts.

The weasels run after you.

Turn to page 32.

22 As Cyril enters the prison, you glance nervously at the guard. He glares at you.

He certainly doesn't look friendly!

You turn away and start to whistle.

Go on to the next page.

A little while later, a tiny old lady comes out of the prison.

"Here, now," says the guard. "It seems to me you were taller when you went in."

The old lady is Toad in disguise!

"Hee, hee." Toad laughs nervously. "I . . ."

Before he can say another word, his ball and chain drops from beneath his skirt!

Turn to page 24.

24   You look down in horror. "Run, Toad!" you cry.

Without wasting another second, you and Toad dash down the street.

Behind you, the guard blows his whistle and yells for help. It won't be long before the whole police force is after you!

You've got to do something fast, but what?

Turn to page 26.

26   You and Toad are heading toward the train station. As you get near it, you can see a motorcar parked there. And on the tracks, an engine is puffing smoke, ready to leave.

Maybe you and Toad should jump aboard the engine. But where will it be going? Maybe you should hide in the motorcar instead.

If you try to board the engine, turn to page 29.

If you hide in the motorcar, turn to page 34.

Another guard leads you and Cyril to Toad's cell.
"Your grandmother is here to see you," he says
to Toad. "And she's brought a friend." Then the
guard leaves.

Toad looks surprised until he sees who his
"grandmother" really is. "Cyril!" he exclaims.

"Shh," warns Cyril. "Here. Put these on," he
says to Toad, showing him a hat and a dress. "You
can escape in this disguise."

Turn to page 28.

After Toad changes, you all tiptoe into the hall.
At once a guard sees you. "Stop!" he yells.
"Come on!" you say. "I remember the way out!"
Toad and Cyril follow you. So does the guard.

But all the halls look alike. Soon you realize that
you *don't* remember the way out! The guard is getting closer, and other guards have joined him.

You turn a corner and stop short. Your escape is
over. The hall you just ran into is a dead . . .

End

You and Toad jump into the cab of the engine.

The engineer, who was oiling the wheels, yells, "Hey! What's going on!"

"We are!" Toad answers, grabbing a switch. "Tallyho!" he cries, as the engine rolls out of the station.

Turn to page 30.

The engine picks up speed and thunders down the track.

"Do you know how to run an engine?" you ask Toad.

"Why, there's nothing to it," he replies. "You just feed it some coal and follow the tracks!"

Somehow you feel there's more to it than that.

"Well, where shall we stop?" you ask.

"Stop?" cries Toad. "I don't know how to *stop*!"

Go on to the next page.

"You don't know how to stop?" you yell. "How
are we going to get off?"

The engine rumbles over a bridge. Toad looks
down at the icy river and cries, "We'll jump!"

"Not me!"

"Well, so long then!" Toad leaps out of the engine
and into the water below.

You look down. You just can't bring yourself to
jump after him.

Turn to page 41.

Mole, Rat, MacBadger, and Toad separate and dash about Toad Hall. They toss the deed back and forth among them, trying to confuse the weasels.

Suddenly the deed drops to the floor.

You're just about to pick it up when two weasels come at you from opposite directions.

Should you stop to pick up the deed or just run?

If you decide to pick up the deed, turn to page 39.

If you decide to run away, turn to page 37.

34　　　You and Toad squeeze down behind the front seat. Suddenly the motorcar starts to roll. The brake must be off!

You jump into the front seat and grab the wheel. You've never driven a car before. What a way to learn!

The road twists and turns. You speed along faster and faster.

"I say! What a grand ride!" yells Toad.

Go on to the next page.

"Grand ride?" you shout back. "We'll be lucky if we get out of this alive!"

You grip the wheel tightly and try to keep the motorcar on the road. Toad stands up and cheers.

You're really moving fast now. Then the road becomes steeper, and you go even *faster*!

"Hang on!" you yell.

Turn to page 36.

Soon the road levels off. Little by little, you slow down. The motorcar comes to a halt at the top of a hill.

"Phew!" you say. "What a ride!"

"It certainly was!" cries Toad. "Let's do it again!"

You shake your head in wonder. No matter what happens, Toad will always be Toad!

The End

As you dart away, the two weasels dive for the deed. But Toad grabs it and runs up the stairs.

The weasels run after him. Quickly Toad folds the deed into a paper airplane. He sails it down to MacBadger—who misses it.

Everyone runs after the plane.

But Toad makes a second plane, and another and another. Winkey and the weasels don't know which one is the deed. There are planes everywhere!

Turn to page 38.

Suddenly you see two planes flying straight toward you, one higher than the other.

"One of those is the deed!" cries Toad. "Grab it!" But which one?

You have to act fast. The planes are heading for the fireplace. If you grab the wrong one, the deed will burn! It will be gone forever. Which one do you grab?

If you grab the higher plane, turn to page 40.

If you grab the lower one, turn to page 42.

You grab the deed just as the two weasels charge at you. You jump back, and they bang into each other instead. Then you yell for your friends to follow you out of Toad Hall.

When you're safe, you hand the deed to Toad.

"Now you can prove that you *did* buy that motorcar," you say. "I hope you've learned a lesson."

"Oh, I have!" replies Toad. "I'm finished with motorcars. I plan to race horses now!"

"Oh, no!" you groan. "Here we go again!"

The End

40   As you grab the higher plane the lower one flies into the fire. You quickly unfold the plane you caught and stare at it in horror. The paper is blank!

The other plane was the deed. Now it's burned to a crisp!

You shake your head. Without the deed, Toad can never prove that he bought the motorcar fair and square! Now he'll have to go back to prison to serve out the rest of his sentence!

The End

You hold on tightly as the engine roars along.

In the distance you see something straight ahead. It's the end of the line! And the engine is traveling faster than ever!

"Oh, no!" you scream. You start pulling switches and turning wheels. The engine slows down a bit. You hope you can stop the engine in time. Otherwise it will be the end of the line for you, too.

The End

You grab the lower plane. The higher one flies into the fire. You unfold the plane you caught—it's the deed!

"I've got it!" you yell to Toad.

"Jolly good!" he cries.

MacBadger calls to the others, "Come on, fellows, we have the deed. Let's be off!"

You hand the deed to Toad and run back into the tunnel with the others.

Go on to the next page.

A few days later, you, Rat, MacBadger, and Mole are celebrating Toad's release.

"By the way," you say, "where *is* Toad?"

Just then, you hear the roar of a motor above the roof of Toad Hall. You rush to the window. It's Toad and Cyril—in an airplane!

You shake your head and sigh. Where will Toad's new adventure end? It looks as though the answer will be left up in the air!

The End